Dear Parents:

Congratulations! Your child is taking the first steps on an exciting journey. The destination? Independent reading!

STEP INTO READING® will help your child get there. The program offers five steps to reading success. Each step includes fun stories and colorful art or photographs. In addition to original fiction and books with favorite characters, there are Step into Reading Non-Fiction Readers, Phonics Readers and Boxed Sets, Sticker Readers, and Comic Readers—a complete literacy program with something to interest every child.

Learning to Read, Step by Step!

Ready to Read   Preschool–Kindergarten
• big type and easy words • rhyme and rhythm • picture clues
For children who know the alphabet and are eager to begin reading.

Reading with Help   Preschool–Grade 1
• basic vocabulary • short sentences • simple stories
For children who recognize familiar words and sound out new words with help.

Reading on Your Own   Grades 1–3
• engaging characters • easy-to-follow plots • popular topics
For children who are ready to read on their own.

Reading Paragraphs   Grades 2–3
• challenging vocabulary • short paragraphs • exciting stories
For newly independent readers who read simple sentences with confidence.

Ready for Chapters   Grades 2–4
• chapters • longer paragraphs • full-color art
For children who want to take the plunge into chapter books but still like colorful pictures.

STEP INTO READING® is designed to give every child a successful reading experience. The grade levels are only guides; children will progress through the steps at their own speed, developing confidence in their reading.

Remember, a lifetime love of reading starts with a single step!

Visit us on the Web!
StepIntoReading.com
rhcbooks.com

Educators and librarians, for a variety of teaching tools, visit us at RHTeachersLibrarians.com

ISBN 978-0-525-64772-0 (trade) — ISBN 978-0-525-64773-7 (lib. bdg.)

Printed in the United States of America

10 9 8 7 6 5 4 3 2 1

nick jr.™

LEMON PIRATES!

by Mary Man-Kong
illustrated by Dave Aikins

Random House 🏠 New York

It is a hot day.

Top Wing cadets

Rod and Brody

go to the Lemon Shack.

They ask Rhonda
for frozen lemon swirlies.
They want to keep cool.

Rhonda is running low
on lemons!
Brody will race
to the Lemon Coast
to get more.

Cap'n Dilly and Matilda
want to make their own
frozen lemon swirlies.
They plan to take
Brody's lemon treasure!

Brody is happy.
He zooms back
to the Lemon Shack
with Rhonda's lemons.

To stop Brody,
Matilda makes holes
in his Splash Wing.

Now Brody's boat
has a leak.
The Splash Wing
is sinking!

Cap'n Dilly and Matilda
take the lemon treasure.
They leave in their
pirate ship.

Brody needs help!
He presses
the Top Wing button
on his watch.

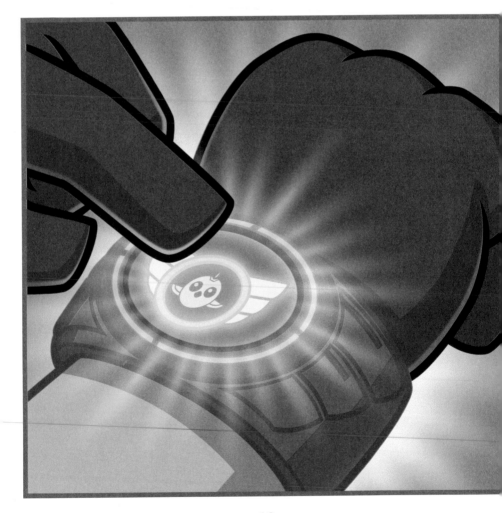

Time for
the Top Wing cadets
to earn their wings!
Penny and Swift will help.

Penny tows
Brody's Splash Wing
to Top Wing Academy's
headquarters.
The boat will get fixed
there.

Swift flies his Flash Wing.
He sees the pirate ship
near some big rocks.

Rod helps, too.

He drives his Road Wing

to the rocks.

But he is too far

from the pirate ship.

Rod has an idea.

With his Road Wing,

he hops from rock to rock

to get to the ship.

He hops right onto the deck.

He cock-a-doodle-*DID* it!

Oh, no!

The pirate ship is heading

for the rocks!

Cap'n Dilly and Matilda

jump off.

Team Top Wing
to the rescue!
Rod steers the ship.

Swift uses his Flash Wing
to move the pirate ship
away from the rocks.
Everyone is safe!

At the Lemon Shack, there are no more lemons to make frozen lemon swirlies.

Top Wing to the rescue!
Rod takes some lemons
to Rhonda
with his Road Wing.

Swift drops some
from his Flash Wing.
Lemons for everyone!

Cap'n Dilly and Matilda
ask nicely for drinks.
Rhonda says yes.
Hooray for Top Wing!
Hooray for frozen lemon
swirlies!